I call my Grandpa

_____

and everyone can see
that I love spending time with him
and he loves being with me.

**For all the wonderful grandfathers I know,
especially Grandpa Klaus and Grandpasaurus Bud.**

Tricycle Press
an imprint of Ten Speed Press
PO Box 7123
Berkeley, California 94707
www.tricyclepress.com

Design by Susan Van Horn
Typeset in Cheltenham
The illustrations in this book were created using gouache and collage.

Library of Congress Cataloging-in-Publication Data

Wolff, Ashley.
I call my grandpa Papa / by Ashley Wolff.
p. cm.
Summary: Students respond, in rhyming text, to their teacher's question
about what each calls his or her grandfather, offering examples of things
they like to do together.
ISBN-13: 978-1-58246-252-3 (hardcover)
ISBN-10: 1-58246-252-6 (hardcover)
[1. Stories in rhyme. 2. Grandfathers–Fiction. 3. Names,
Personal–Fiction.] I. Title.
PZ8.3.W843Iad 2009
[E]–dc22

2008042184

First Tricycle Press printing, 2009
Printed in Singapore

1 2 3 4 5 6 — 13 12 11 10 09

I Call My Grandpa Papa

by

ASHLEY WOLFF

TRICYCLE PRESS
Berkeley / Toronto

"My grandfather from China
is visiting today.
Class, please welcome **Ye-Ye**!"
said Miss Alexandra May.

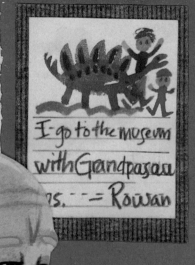

"Our grandpas all have stories—
no two are just the same.
They have so much to teach us
and deserve their special names.

Will you please tell Ye-Ye
about these pictures that you drew
of you and all your grandpas
and what you love to do?"

Grandpa likes
the Ferris wheel.
——— —David

My Abuelo likes
to swim with me.
—Cesar

Dad
two

Cesar said, "Let me go first!
See us swimming in the pool?
My **Abuelo** taught me
   how to dive.
I think he's really cool!"

My Abuelo likes
to swim with me.

"I wear boots just like my **Papi**'s.
When we go for a walk,
we identify each bug and tree
and lift up every rock."

"I really love the Tilt-A-Whirl, but **Grandpa**'s favorite ride is high up on the Ferris Wheel— with me right by his side!"

"My **Daddo** has two horses:
Napoleon and Dot.
As soon as I can giddy-up,
he'll teach me how to trot!"

"My **Dedushka** is amazing. He can make things disappear, and once he found a quarter right behind my ear!"

"**Nonno** takes me to his barbershop.
We sit in two big chairs,
and a nice man named Rosario
cuts off all our hair."

TYRANNOSAURUS REX *(tyrant reptile)* had a massive head, lethal serrated teeth, arms capable of lifting hundreds of pounds, and sharp claws on its birdlike feet and two-fingered hands. *50 feet long.*

PACHYCEPHALOSAURUS *(thick-headed reptile)* honked and bellowed as it ran on its two feet across highland areas. *26 feet long.*

STEGOSAURUS *(roofed reptile)* might have used the bony plates on its back to keep its body cool—like big ears on an elephant do. *30 feet long.*

"**Grandpasaurus** follows me.
We can't wait to see them:
Tyrannosaurs and raptors
live here—in the museum!"

PTERANODON (*winged and toothless*) was a fur-covered, flying reptile who soared over the sea, collecting fish in a pelican-like pouch. *26 feet long.*

TRICERATOPS (*three-horned face*) was a plant eater protected by an armory of horns and neck shields. *30 feet long.*

DEINONYCHUS (*terrible claw*) was a fast runner who leaped into the air to attack prey. *13 feet long.*

"This is **Bapa**'s woodshop.
He lets me use his tools
if I wear ALL my safety gear
and follow his shop rules."

"**Ojii-San** is tall and strong.
He lifts me way up high
so I can see the whole parade
as it goes marching by!"

"My **Pops** likes playing catch with me.
He gave me his old glove,
but cheering for my baseball team
is what he really loves."

"My **Babu** runs the library.
He can check out any book,
and when he gets the new ones,
he lets me have first look."

"I don't really have a Grandpa—
Pappous died when I was three.
But my next-door neighbor, Mr. Tran,
is **Papa-T** to me."

"My **Opa** took me camping,
and the part I loved the most
was eating the marshmallows
he taught me how to toast."

"I call my Grandpa **Papa**.
I feel safest in his lap
when we see the
lightning flash
and hear the
thunder clap!"

Papa likes to watch
thunder storms
with me. -Tessa

"Thank you, Tessa," said Miss May,
"and thank you everyone
for telling us your grandpa's name,
and what you do for fun.

CHINA

 pa likes to watch
under storms
with me. =Tessa

go to the museu
with Grandpasau

You are their precious young ones,
and I can guarantee
that they'll love you just as dearly...

when you're all grown up,

like me!"